P9-DCG-455

Hunting the White Cow

story by TRES SEYMOUR
pictures by
WENDY ANDERSON HALPERIN

Orchard Books   New York

Thanks to the staff of the Extrom Photographic Archives of the University of Kentucky in
Louisville for their generous help with the historical research. —W.A.H.

Text copyright © 1993 by Tres Seymour
Illustrations copyright © 1993 by Wendy Anderson Halperin

Orchard Books, 95 Madison Avenue, New York, NY 10016

Manufactured in the United States of America. Printed by Barton Press, Inc.
Bound by Horowitz/Rae. Book design by Mina Greenstein.
The text of this book is set in 15 point Scotch Roman. The illustrations are pencil and watercolor reproduced
in full color. 10 9 8 7 6 5 4 3 2 1

Library of Congress Cataloging-in-Publication Data
Seymour, Tres. Hunting the white cow / story by Tres Seymour ; pictures by Wendy Anderson Halperin.   p.   cm.
"A Richard Jackson book." Summary: A child watches as more and more people join in the attempts to catch the family
cow that has gotten loose, each remarking on how special the cow is.
ISBN 0-531-05496-9 ISBN 0-531-08646-1 (lib. bdg.)
[1. Cows—Fiction.] I. Halperin, Wendy Anderson, ill.
II. Title. PZ7.S5253Hu 1993 [E]—dc20 92-43757

To my father and my grandfather

—T.S.

For my parents, Haas and Andy

—W.A.H.

Somewhere north of Priceville there's a white cow nobody can catch.

She used to be ours, but she went wild.

When she first got loose, Mr. Matthew, who helps
Daddy run the farm, said, "Let's get a rope and go catch
that buster."

So he and Daddy put on their overalls and feed caps and
pulled up their old, brown, crusty cow-pie boots and got into
the orange pickup truck to hunt the white cow.

"Can I come?" I asked, but Daddy said no, they'd be back in a few minutes.

I woke up when they came stomping on the porch around midnight.

Mr. Matthew had mud all up and down one side, and Daddy had lost his feed cap. Mama plucked the leaves out of his hair.   They didn't catch the white cow.

"I tell you what," said Mr. Matthew. "That cow is one tough dude."

"I always said she was smart," said Daddy. "Smartest cow in the county."

That cow was so smart she kept hid for weeks. The next
we heard of her was when Ollie Jarboe, who owns the store,

called on the phone and said, "Y'all's white cow is in Wilson's tobacco patch."

This time Daddy called up Uncle Bill and Uncle Bob to help hunt the white cow. They drove up with their overalls and feed caps and cow-pie boots already on and ready to go.

"Can I come?" I asked, but Uncle Bill said it would only take them half an hour.

"I'll believe that when I see it," said Mama.

They missed dinner. Daddy had so many stick-tites stuck to him he looked plumb green. Uncle Bob groaned and rubbed his legs where he'd run through a patch of saw briers. All four smelled like they'd rolled in tobacco.

"I tell you what," said Mr. Matthew. "That cow is one tough dude."

"And smart," said Daddy. "Smartest cow in the county."

"And fat, I reckon!" said Uncle Bill. "Lord, what a cow."

"She always had a pretty calf," said Uncle Bob. "You got a fine cow there."

"If you can ever catch her," said Mama.

We never did see the white cow again for a month, but then Ollie Jarboe called and said, "Y'all's cow is in Horton's cornfield, eating like an old sow."

Daddy took no chances. He called Papaw to come help him and Mr. Matthew and Uncle Bill and Uncle Bob hunt the white cow. Papaw wore the crustiest cow-pie boots I ever saw.

"Can I come?" I asked, but Papaw said they'd only be gone an hour and a half. They had a secret weapon.

Papaw was the best cow-caller in southern Kentucky. He'd holler, "SOUK! SOUK! SOUK! SOUK-EF! WHEEEEOO! SOUK!" and every cow for miles would moo and follow him like a dog. They'd get the white cow for sure.

They didn't catch the white cow. Mama had to help wring Daddy out from falling in the creek. Mr. Matthew shook the corn out of his boots. Uncle Bob picked the dirt out of his teeth with a toothpick, and Papaw and Uncle Bill took turns rubbing each other's knees.

"I tell you what," said Mr. Matthew. "That cow is one tough dude."

"And smart," said Daddy.

"And fat, I reckon!" said Uncle Bill.

"She always had a pretty calf, I recollect," said
Uncle Bob.

"And the sweetest milk you ever tasted," Papaw said.

"That cow's never been milked in her life," said Mama.
Nobody paid her any mind.

We never did see that cow again till I saw her myself. I'd
spent the day in the woods, and just about dusk I spied her
in the top pasture. I stalked up quiet-like. I could hear her

tearing up the grass and munching it into a cud, and
breathing heavy like cows do, and switching her tail in the
warm air. I could almost touch her when she looked right
at me.

But she didn't run. She let me lead her by the old rope around her neck till we got to the woods. Then she stopped. "Cow," I said, "I ain't letting go of this rope."

She looked at me as if to say, "I ain't going no farther." Well, I wasn't about to let go of the famous white cow. "You ain't so smart," I said. "Daddy will come looking for me and see that I caught you and brag on me something awful."

I waited a while, and it got dark. I waited a while more and I got sleepy.

I leaned up against a stump with the rope tied around my wrist so that old cow couldn't go anywhere.

Well, guess what. I didn't catch the white cow. Daddy
found me asleep by the stump, but that old cow had just
wrapped the rope around a tree and broken it off.

When I got home, everybody had something to say.

"I tell you what," Mr. Matthew said. "That cow is one tough dude."

"And smart," said Daddy.

"And fat, I reckon!" said Uncle Bill.

"She always had a pretty calf," said Uncle Bob.
"And the sweetest milk you ever tasted," said Papaw.
I didn't say anything. But I did keep the white cow's
rope, and it's held up my pants ever since.

Papaw's going to teach me cow-calling. Watch out, white cow. Watch out.